COWBOYS

VOICES IN THE WESTERN WIND

Poems by **David L. Harrison**

Illustrations by **Dan Burr**

WORDƒONG

Honesdale, PA

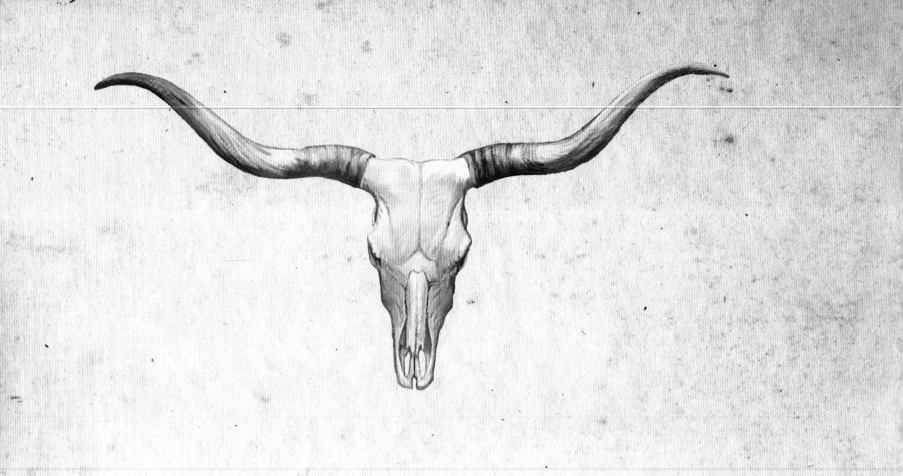

Wordsong
An Imprint of Boyds Mills Press, Inc.
815 Church Street
Honesdale, Pennsylvania 18431
Printed in China

ISBN: 978-1-59078-877-6
Library of Congress Control Number: 2011939946

First edition
The text of this book is set in Goudy Old Style.
The illustrations are digital paintings.

10 9 8 7 6 5 4 3 2 1

For Tim, my favorite son-in-law
                              —DLH

To the cowboys and cattlemen of the Teton Valley,
my friends and neighbors,
with thanks and gratitude to be among you
                              —DB

SIGN ME UP

Every year I say I'm quit,
had my fill'a drivin' cows to Abilene.
Sign me up again?
I reckon not.

Had enough of the Chisholm Trail—
dust, fly bites, saddle sores—
I'd be plumb loco
to sign again.

Last time: a longhorn busted my leg,
had three stampedes,
a cranky boss,
bellyache prett' near every night
from Cookie's cookin'.
Don't know, really,
what else I'd do.

Man can think
out there on the prairie,
lyin' at night by a good fire,
swappin' stories,
lookin' at stars.

Don't know, really,
what else I'd do.

Aw, sign me up.

DRESSED FOR WORK

Two months' pay in these boots,
but they aren't just boots.
They're special made—
soft, tight
to keep my feet small—
not like clodhopper farm-boys' feet
kickin' in the dirt.
No sir!

This hat?
Four months' pay.
You try with less
when the sun'll melt a rock
or it's rainin' to choke a toad
while you're out chasin' strays.

You need sand in your gizzard
to wrangle wild cows,
chaps for fendin' off thorns
or horses with a taste
for cowpoke leg.

I wear a vest with deep pockets
to hold my tally book and such,
a good bandanna for keepin' out dust
or, say, I get bit by a durn rattler
and have to tie up my arm.

Takes spurs, gloves, long johns—
a cowboy's covered head to toe.
Those knights in armor
thought they were tough,
but I'll tell you what:
they never got horned by a steer,
dragged by a horse,
or tangled with the likes of me!

BRANDED

Go on and beller, little feller.
Beller 'cause it hurts and stinks.
But things ain't so bad.
Mama's fixin' to lick your face,
make you feel better.

Some days I could beller myself,
only boss don't cotton
to crybaby cowboys,
and I'm a fur piece from home.

Things go right,
maybe we'll meet
on the trail by and by,
both of us doin'
what we have to.

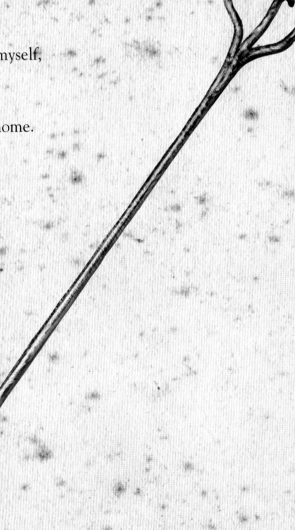

THE BUNKHOUSE

Reckon this place could use a cleanin'.
Some boys hang their clothes on the floor
so they can't fall off nuthin',
and I've seen more'n one jaw of juice
fail to make it plumb out the door.

The walls are purty good,
got mostly recent papers pasted on.
Helps keep out wind in winter
while we catch up on the latest news.

It's nice to have a bunkhouse
in case you're partial to smellin' sweat,
boots trackin' cow manure,
and lamps burnin' skunk-fat oil.

Mighty warm in summer, though.
Good part is
the snakes eat the rats,
but the stink'll make your eyes water some.

Don't much care for sleepin' in.
Bugs gnaw plugs right outta your hide.
Reckon that's why I spread my roll outdoors.

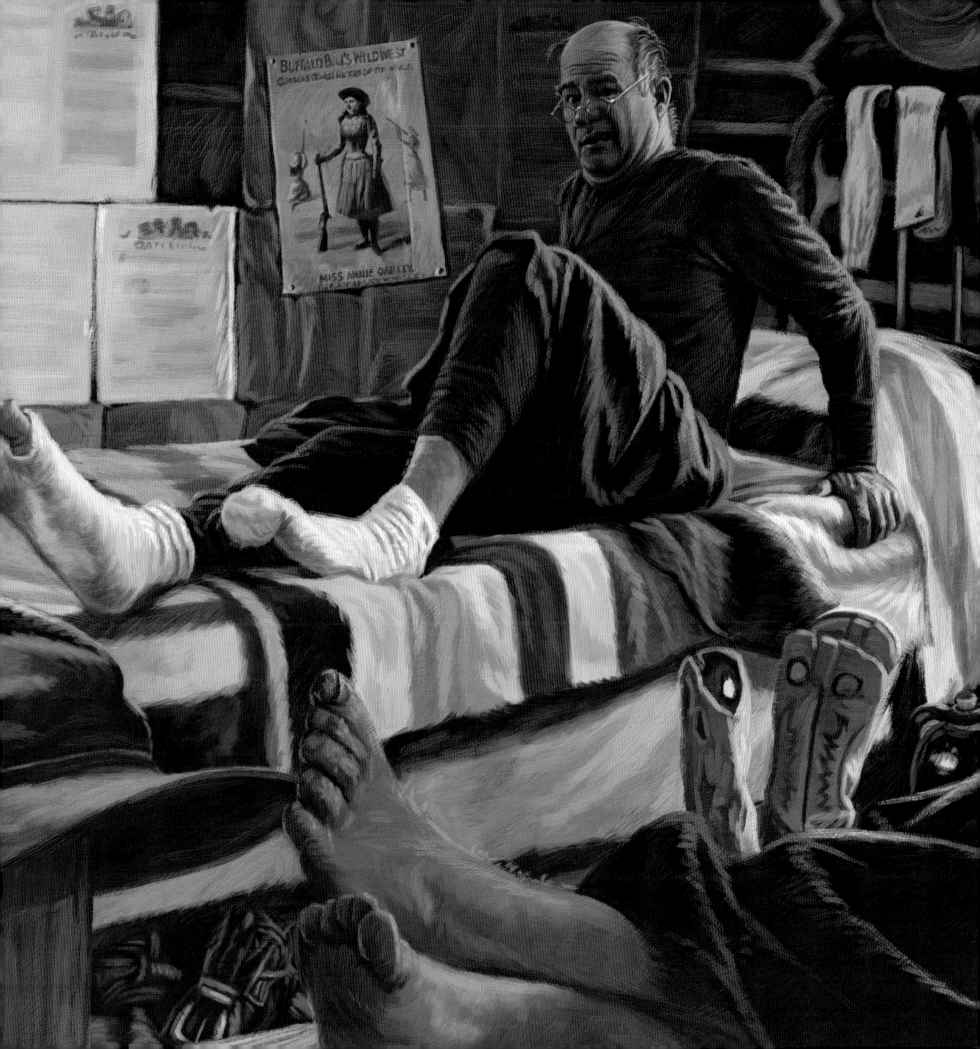

SPITTIN' MAD

Not fair!

"You're too little," they say.
"Go play with your dolls."

Been ridin' since I could walk.
I could break a bronco
good as they can.

"You're a girl," they say.
"Stay out of the way."

I'm tougher'n any boy.
Mess with me,
I'll poke 'em in the eye!

Not fair.

Not fair!

I'm so mad
I could kick a cow chip!

Not!

Fair!

MENDING FENCE

Twelve miles of fence
stretched in a line
like a pencil drawing out my future.

Sorry things happen to a fence.
Takes some doing to string barbed wire
where something big busted out, or in.
Sometimes a longhorn tangles up,
dies before I find it.

Winter wire freezes fingers,
summer wire burns blisters.
Wind? Son, it's always here,
whistling in your ears,
doing its best
to talk you out of your hat.

Expect what you don't expect
along a fencerow.
I've pulled porcupine quills
from noses of bawling calves,
lassoed steers stuck in bogs,
out of their minds from biting flies.

Some might reckon mending fence is simple.
Son, they just don't know.
Twelve miles is a long spell from supper,
and out here it's sky, the fence, and me.

CHASING A STRAY

Dang!
There goes another one.

Worse'n some fool kid
chasin' rabbits.

No you don't, you loco cow!
I'll skin your ornery hide!

You get back here!
Huh! Huh! Huh! Huh!

Don't you shake those horns at me.
Cook'll turn you into chili!

Now you hear me?

Huh! Huh!

That's better.

MAKES PERFECT

First cowboy

Ha!
You missed that can a mile!
Lucky that post's no grizzly bear.
You'd be lunch by now.

Ha!
My granny's quicker'n you
and she's eighty!
Reckon that grizz'd
be pickin' his teeth by now.

Nah.
Hope I never do.

I just saved
your sorry hide
from a grizz!

Let's eat.

Second cowboy

Ha yourself.
I'm better'n you.
And quicker!

Ever see a real gunfight?
Curly says he saw one once
in Abilene.

Hey!
You hit the can!

I'd'a got him
next shot.

Let's eat.

SETTING OUT

All my life,
do what Master say.
He say, "Mind my cows,"
I mind his cows.

Cows, me,
my children,
wife—
all his.

No more.
Nobody owns me now.
Signed my X,
agreed to drive this rancher's cows
from Texas up to Abilene—

for pay.
My pay.

I'm on a journey of my own
figuring how it feels
to be free.

MEETING THE BOSS

Listen up, boys,
here's how it is.
You're paid to drive these cows
to Abilene.
I'm paid to see you do.
Any questions?

It's a far piece to Abilene,
with three thousand head of cows
strung for miles along the trail.
We walk 'em by day,
bed 'em by night.
Any questions?

Cookie'll be your best friend.
He'll cook your food,
tend to bites and bellyaches,
play a little music now and then.
I recommend don't break a bone,
but if you do,
he'll set it if he can.

Last year we had the pleasure
of back-to-back stampedes.
One boy got his leg broke.
Cookie did his best.
It wasn't easy.
Any questions?

No whiskey, guns,
or knives in camp.
Cookie keeps a rifle,
so do I.
Fighting is against the rules.
Spurs are not for gouging.
No yanking hair,
kicking, biting—
do, you'll answer to me.

Tonight will be your last bath
'tween here and Abilene.
I'm telling you, boys,
that's how it will be.
Got problems,
bring them to me.
Any questions?

HEADED TO ABILENE

First day out, fifteen miles,
one thousand miles to go.

One thousand miles
of burnin' sun,
swollen rivers,
stampedes, wolves,
three thousand cows,
fifteen men,
one thousand miles to go.

Up from Texas headed north,
next hot bath two months away.
Half-wild longhorns graze the trail,
not too fast, not too slow,
cows are money, pounds are dollars,
make the rancher rich and happy,
one thousand miles to go.

Someone has to walk these critters,
lead the way, guard their rear.
Someone has to round up strays,
watch for danger in the night,
work till horse and rider drop,
one thousand miles to go.

From Texas through the Indian lands
clear to Abilene.
We can't wait to get there,
and we've only just begun.

SNAKE!

Rattlesnake!

Watch it!

Hey! Hey!
Settle down!

Settle down!

Loco pony!

You'll kill us both!

Next time
I'll throw a saddle
on the snake!

PRAIRIE NEWS

First cowboy

See 'em?

Somethin's dead.

Bet a grizz made a kill.

Else they'd land.

Find out who the feller was?

Think we ought to ride out?

Can't leave these cows.

Nothin' to us.

Yeah.

Second cowboy

Reckon
there must be twenty.

Somethin' big
to draw that many.

Bet he's there.

One time,
found a skeleton,
picked clean,
down to the boots.

Nope. Just buried him,
bones and boots.

See what's there?

Just as well.

Still, you wonder.

You kind'a do.

COOKIE

Tonight's your lucky night, boys.
Look what I fixed for you!
Stood all day in the burning sun
to make this son-of-a-gun stew.

Longhorn steaks two inches thick,
dig in while they're hot.
The coffee'll keep you up all night,
belly up to the pot.

You know your Cookie loves you, boys,
loves to see you fed.
Stood all day in the burning sun
to bake this sourdough bread.

Sop up all the stew, boys,
take another steak.
Have another hunk of bread.
You know I love to bake.

You know your Cookie loves you, boys,
tell you what I'll do—
tomorrow I'll fix steak and bread
and a big old pot of stew!

COLD RAIN

Makes me wonder
what I'm doin' here
freezin' in my saddle,
teeth chatterin' like dice
on a barroom table.

Makes me wonder
why I left home
to live like this—
throwin' ropes at cows,
dodgin' rattlers,
driftin' like tumbleweed
blown on the wind. . . .

I feel cold enough to die.
Makes me wonder why.

THOSE STARS

Those stars—
those stars make a man
lie here and think.

I'm tired to my bones
from chasin' beeves
outta dead-end gullies,

got boils where boils
shouldn't oughtta be,

can't hardly remember
bein' clean.

But those stars,
they look down
like heaven's own eyes.

I think they're sayin'
my little cares
don't 'mount up to much,

and tomorrow—
tomorrow's comin'
either way.

TROUBLE
COMING

Wind's up.
Don't like those clouds
fingering down.

Could be anything.
Twister maybe.
Nothing good.

Cows are restless.
Sniffing the air.
First lightning, thunder,
they'll run.

Some of these boys
don't know
what it's like.

Got a bad feeling
about this night.

STAMPEDE!

Gotta stop 'em . . . can't . . . see . . . rain
. . . dark . . . hooves . . . thunder . . . don't
go down . . . ground slick . . . don't go
. . . down . . . find the . . . find the . . .
find the front . . . gotta turn 'em! . . .
ground . . . shakin' . . . don't go . . . down
. . . dead man . . . if I fall . . . hooves . . .
horns . . . can't see! . . . dead man if I fall!

ABILENE

Watch 'em, boys, watch 'em.
They'll pour through town
like muddy water,
churn those streets to brown mush.

Sooner we get these beeves sold,
sooner we get our pay, boys,
sooner we hit the trail.

First I want a hot bath
to soak this ornery stink
outta my bones.

I want a bed,
I want some fun.

Then
I'm headed home.

BRINGIN' 'EM IN

First cowboy

Hey Tom,
watch the kid.

You'd think he brought
these cows to town
by himself.

Reminds me of me
at his age—
proud to finish
my first drive.

Ain't you?

Second cowboy

Chest puffed out
like a banty rooster.

Full'a sass,
tryin' to impress the ladies.

Still tryin'
to impress the ladies?

THE LESSON

No.
Not again.

Can't believe my stinkin' luck.

They cleaned me out.
What am I going to do?

Pair'a jacks beat my tens.
Should'a folded.
Not me!
What am I going to do?

When will I learn to stay out of card games?
Save my money?
Take it home?

A thousand miles drivin' beeves,
eighty dollars—
gone

gone

to a pair of jacks.

Lost it all.

Eighty dollars.

What am I going to do?

THE RACE

First cowboy	Second cowboy
Bet you we can beat that train.	
	Bet we can.
Coal burner,	
	Belchin' smoke.
Puffin' like an old man.	
	Can't outrun a horse like mine.
Hey, train!	
	Eat our dust!
Whoa, train.	
	What's your hurry?
Hey, train.	
	What's the rush?
Well,	
	We beat it . . .
for a while.	for a while.

WHO WERE THE COWBOYS?

William Henry Wakefield was born in Wilsey, Kansas, in 1878. His father was a hard man who beat his sons. By the time Bill was four, he was sleeping on the ground to guard his father's cattle. A neighbor said a little boy shouldn't be treated that way. "Did my son complain to you?" asked Mr. Wakefield. "No," said the neighbor. "Mind your own business," said Mr. Wakefield. Bill grew up tough in a tough family. At fourteen, he'd had enough. He left home and became a cowboy.

Many cowboys were young—in their teens or early twenties. Many had stories like Bill Wakefield's. Some of them were white; some were black, including former slaves. A lot were Mexicans. Some of the best were Indians. Civil War veterans and ex-railroad workers became cowboys. So did immigrants and sons of immigrants.

After the Civil War ended in 1865, Texas ranchers raised huge herds of longhorns. People in New York and other eastern cities liked their beef. A cow worth four dollars in West Texas might bring forty dollars at market. The problem for ranchers was how could they get their cattle to market? The nearest railhead that could ship cows to the Chicago stockyards was hundreds of miles away. There was only one way to get the longhorns there: walk.

Longhorns grew up half-wild, roaming for miles across the rugged range. Big ones weighed a ton, with sharp horns eight feet wide from tip to tip. Taking herds of these animals across open prairies from Texas up through Indian country (Oklahoma) into Kansas, with its booming "cow towns" such as Abilene, Dodge City, or Wichita, took gutsy men. The trip could take two or three months of hard, sweaty work, sleeping on the ground and eating mostly beef and beans.

The cowboys signed on to this life. They were men with grit, hired by ranchers for a dollar a day and a place to eat and sleep.

From 1866 to 1886, an estimated 40,000 cowboys drove 10 million or more longhorns to market. Then, almost as suddenly as it began, the cattle drive became part of history. Pioneers by the thousands were streaming west. Many established their farms along famous cattle-drive trails such as the Chisholm Trail and fenced off their land to protect their crops. Railheads for shipping cattle kept moving farther west, closer to the herds. Meat-packing plants sprang up, making it unnecessary to ship cows at all. Meat could be shipped in refrigerated train cars instead. An era had come to an end.

On one of the last big drives, Bill Wakefield's trail boss leaned forward in his saddle to gaze at the sea of longhorn cattle spread before them. "Take a good look," he told Bill. "You won't see this again."

—DLH